WHISPERS OF FIREFLIES

By Queeny Yalangi

FanatiXx® Publication

FanatiXx® Publication

Rourkela | Mumbai | Delhi NCR | Ahmedabad

Whispers Of Fireflies
By Queeny Yalangi

ISBN: 978-93-7406-424-5
MRP: Rs. 299 / $15

First Edition – 2025

For permissions, inquiries, or feedback:
Email: outreach@fanatixx.info
Instagram: @fanatixxpublication

This Book is for all the readers across the globe who read, reviewed, and loved my debut book Life in Hyderabad a city of tales. Your love and warmth always reminds me of why I started this journey. Thank you for believing in me and giving me a space in your hearts. I hope you love this book too!

Mom this one is for you ♡

This book is for every girl who ever self-doubt her worth,
for every girl who felt like she's not enough,

for every girl who was told she's not perfect,
for every girl who was told that she's not beautiful,

for every girl who was told that she's nothing,
for every girl who was disrespected,

for every girl who was told not to laugh loud,
for every girl whose voice was silenced,

for every girl who was told to be in her limits,
for every girl who was told she knew nothing,

for every girl who was told to adjust,
for every girl who was not given a choice,

for every girl who was told she's too much,
for every girl who sacrificed her dreams,

for every girl who lived in pain,
for every girl who cried alone,

for every girl who was bullied,
for every girl who was abused,

for every girl who was scared,
for every girl who lost herself,

for every girl who felt unloved,
for every girl who lost hope,

for every girl who dies everyday thousand times inside,

but walks towards her future by keeping one foot in front of the other. Girl, this one is for you and I'm sorry if this world made you feel that way. You are stronger than you think and you are beautiful just the way you are. You are worthy of every good thing in this world as much as we all are. You deserve all the love in this world as much as we are.

And You deserve all the respect in this world as much as we are. If anyone else says otherwise, then they are lying to you. You are stronger than everything that's weighing you down. You are so brave. Just open your wings and chase your dreams. Don't let anyone stop you. Because this life is yours and you get to live it only once, so choose what you want. I hope this book helps you find the light you are searching for.

I know there are many Carols out there who are confused, who makes mistakes and who has lots of questions in mind and they don't know whom to ask or whom to discuss with. I hope you all can relate to Carol and I hope Amber and Pearl answers all your questions and helps you navigate through life challenges. I want you all to know that I love you and I want you to love yourself. Because, there's no greater strength in this world than Self-love. I hope my book "Whispers of Fireflies" makes you all fall in love with yourselves again.

I wish you all hope, love, light and healing,
Queeny Yalangi.

CONTENTS

STORY 1: SELF-DOUBT

Carol: "Do you think I'm beautiful?"

Pearl: "Yes, you are."

Amber: "You are the most beautiful girl I ever met."

Carol: "Is it true?"

Pearl: "Yes, it's true, you are beautiful my love."

Carol: "Why no one ever told me this?"

Amber: "It's okay Carol, you know it now."

Carol: "Isn't it too late?" (worried)

Pearl: "No, it isn't."

Amber: "There is no right or wrong time to know you are beautiful."

Carol: "But..... I'm scared. What if people find me ugly?" (sighs)

Pearl: "No Carol, you don't need other's opinion."

Amber: "Yes, you just have to love yourself just the way you are."

Carol: "So, that's enough?

Pearl: "Yes, that's enough?"

Amber: "You know, Mom says 'If you believe you are beautiful, then you are beautiful. You just have to love yourself first, inside and out, before anyone loves you.'"

Carol: "So it all depends on me?"

Pearl: "Yes, it is."

Carol: "So I just have to love myself first?"

Amber: "Yes. But remember, even before someone does."

Carol: "Wow, I get it now. You guys are so confident because you always love yourselves first and you don't wait for someone to do that for you."

Pearl: "You got it right gal."

Amber: "Absolutely."

Carol: "Thank you Pearl and Amber for helping me out. I now know I'm beautiful and I'll love myself more and more here after."

Pearl: "Yippee."

Amber: "You go gal."
(Everyone hugs)

STORY 2: KINDNESS

Carol: "What is the best thing I can do for myself?"

Pearl: "Be kind to yourself."

Carol: "How can I be kind to myself?"

Amber: "It's simple. You just have to treat yourself just the way you treat others with respect and kindness."

Carol: "Yes, I do treat others with respect and kindness. But how can I treat myself in the same way."

Pearl: "Let me tell you a secret, Carol." (whispers)

Carol: "Okay. What is it?"

Pearl: "We always take care of others, but we often forget to take care of ourselves and we push ourselves to be better and to do better all the time."

Pearl: "And we always be hard on ourselves for not achieving greater things."

Amber: "And we feel guilty for not living up to someone's expectations."

Pearl: "And for not being perfect."

Amber: "For not being the best."

Carol: "Yes, it happens with me all the time."

Pearl: "Yes, it happens with everyone."

Amber: "And when it happens we all forget our true selves and become someone new and different."

Carol: "Does that mean we lose ourselves?"

Pearl: "Of course, we lose ourselves in the race."

Carol: "So what should I do then?"

Amber: "You should be kind to yourself first."

Pearl: "You shouldn't hurt yourself for not being the best in the room."

Amber: "And you have to stop trying to be the best all the time."

Pearl: "You should treat yourself with same respect you treat others."

Amber: "You shouldn't carry the weight of someone's dreams on your shoulders."

Pearl: "You just have to work hard for your dreams and your life."

Carol: "Doesn't that make me bad?"

Pearl: “No my dear.”

Amber: “You know mom always says that we should always be kind to ourselves and treat ourselves with the same love we give others.”

Pearl: ”That’s how we become kind and empathetic.”

Carol: “Okay. I will start being kind to myself from this moment on. You guys are true friends and I love you both.” (Carol jumps on them as they sit and talk happily)

STORY 3: SELF-LOVE

Carol: “What is Self-love?”

Pearl: “I know about it.”

Carol: “What is it?”

Pearl: “But I’m not going to tell you.”

Carol: “Why?”

Pearl: “Because you broke my pink lipstick.”

Carol: “I dropped it on the floor while I was applying it.”

Pearl: “You didn’t tell me until I asked about it.”

Carol: “I thought you won’t feel bad about it because we are friends.”

Pearl: “I will feel bad about it because it’s my favorite lipstick and you broke it and you don’t even feel sorry about it.”

Carol: “Why didn’t you tell me this before?”

Pearl: “Because you never asked me.”

Carol: "You should have told me" (tears in eyes)

Pearl: "Like I said before, you never asked me about it."

Amber: "Hey girls, you two don't fight. Carol, can you come here once?"

(Carol walks slowly to Amber and sits in front of her on knees)

Amber:" Now tell me what do you want to know?" (asks while holding her hands)

Carol: "Pearl knows about Self-love. But she is not telling me, because I broke her lipstick."

Amber: "Hahaha! Is that why you both fighting?"

Carol: "Yes." (says with sad face)

Amber: "I will tell you about self-love, but promise me you will not fight with Pearl again."

Carol: "Okay, done."

Amber: "Self-love is secret ingredient to a happy life."

Carol: "Is it?"

Amber: "Yes, it is an Elixir."

Carol: Whaaaaaat! An Elixirrrrrr!

Amber: "Yes Carol, and it is important in everyone's life. Everyone should have that Self-love inside them to be strong and independent."

Carol: "Isn't it selfish to love ourselves?"

Amber: "No it isn't. It gives hope."

Carol: "Hope? That's interesting."

Amber: "Self-love is something where you water yourself before you water someone else. Where you be there for yourself, before being there for someone. Where you take care of yourself, before you take care of others. Where you love yourself, before you love others."

Carol: "Tell me more."

Amber: "You can feel that self-love when you believe in yourself before someone else believes in you. When you love yourself before someone else loves you. When you become your best friend before someone else becomes your friend. It tells you what is good for you, what is bad for you. It helps you differentiate between right and wrong. It tells you what to hold and what to let go. It tells you when to stay and when to let go. It tells you what is fair and what is not."

Carol: "How I can find it inside me?"

Amber: "You don't have to find it, it is already there within you. You just have to practice it everyday."

Carol: "Okay, how is it going to help me?"

Amber: “It makes you confident in life, It helps you to put yourself first, it helps you to make the right decisions, right choices, and It helps you to be good to yourself.”

Carol: “It sounds cool.”

Amber: “Yes, it is cool.”

Carol: “Do you believe in Self-love?”

Amber: “Yes I do. You know, mom says, 'Self-love is something that keeps you going in life, even when there's no one to support you, even when there's no one to love you, and even when there's no one to embrace you.'"

Carol: “That means I can become strong if I have self-love?”

Amber: “Yes, you can.”

Carol: “Then I’m going to practice Self-love everyday.”

Amber: “Now go and make peace with Pearl, remember you broke her lipstick and you know it’s a bad thing right.”

Carol: “Yes, I know.”
(Carol goes to Pearl)

Carol: “I’m sorry pearl.”

Pearl: “That’s okay, Carol.”

Carol: “Can you forgive me?”

Pearl: “Yes. Only if you promise me that you will never break my lipsticks again.”

Carol: "Pinky promise."(Both laughs and hugs each other. Amber joins them)

STORY 4: PERFECTION

Carol: "Am I perfect?"

Pearl: "There's no such thing as perfection, Carol."

Amber: "Yes Carol, Pearl is right."

Carol: "But guys everyone loves perfection, and nobody will love me if I'm not perfect."

Pearl: "That's not true Carol."

Amber: "You don't have to be perfect to be loved by someone."

Carol: "But it matters right.?"

Pearl: "No Carol, you got it wrong. There isn't such thing as Perfection. It's all a lie."

Amber: "Yes, it's a lie. We all have flaws and we become who we are because of our flaws, when we own them, when we embrace them without any shame."

Carol: "Is it? But people don't like flaws right."

Pearl: "Don't bother about what others like in you, Carol. Think about what you like about yourself."

Carol: "I don't like being flawed person. I want to be perfect."

Amber: "Your flaws are your identity Carol. You learn through your flaws and mistakes. It's a step by step process in becoming your true self."

Carol: "True self?"

Pearl: "Yes, True self is a space inside you where you accept your good and bad side, where you accept your wins and losses, where you accept your highs and lows, where you accept that you become something even when you don't have anything. It is where you choose what you want to become and who you want to become. It is where you decide what you want, without any regrets, any guilt and any shame. Just accepting everything that is happening in and around you."

Carol: "Aw, it is very amusing. Tell me more."

Amber: "You know, mom says we all are perfect just the way we are, and we have to embrace our imperfections to be happy in life."

Pearl: "Yes we have to embrace our imperfections and shouldn't hide them from the world."

Carol: "What happens if I hide them?"

Pearl: "Then you won't be happy and peaceful, Carol. If you act as someone else who is perfect then you lose yourself forever. You will lose your identity and you will be remembered as someone else and not you."

Carol: "Then what's the solution for this?"

Pearl: "Stop trying to be perfect in everything Carol."

Amber: "Just be who you are and embrace all your imperfections with all your heart. Because, if you don't like yourself with all your flaws, then no one is going to do that for you. Just try to become a better person and not perfect person than you were yesterday. That's how you keep evolving and that is all matters."

Carol: "Thank you Amber. You are the best. " (Carol hugs Amber as they see their reflection in water)

STORY 5: LOVE

Carol: "What is love?"

Pearl: "It's magic."

Carol: "Magic?"

Amber: "Yes Carol."

Carol: "How can we see it?"

Pearl: "We can't see it Carol, we can only just feel it."

Amber: "It's everywhere around you, even it's there inside you. You just have to feel it in your heart."

Carol: "Okay, I'm feeling it. Feeeeeeeeling itttttttt. Wait, stop. I still don't see it guys. I don't feel it. Maybe I don't have it inside me."

Pearl: "It's not like that Carol.

Amber: "There's love inside you. When you care about your friends and family, when you protect them, when you be there for them, when you take stand for them. That's love."

Carol: "Yes, I do that."

Pearl: “Then there’s love inside you, you just don’t know it.”

Amber: “You know, Mom says ‘Love is something that makes you want to come home every day.’”

Carol: “Maybe that’s why I just come to you guys no matter where I’m. And everything feels better when I’m around you.”

Pearl: “See. That’s Love.”

Amber: “Love is something that makes you feel complete, it gives you freedom, it makes you strong from the inside, it makes you confident, it makes you brave.”

Carol: “ So that’s love?”

Pearl: “Yes, my dear.”

Amber: “ Love is that abode where you feel safe in someone’s arms. Where you trust someone with all your heart.”

Carol: “That means only I should trust them?”

Pearl: “No Carol, they should also trust you.”

Amber: “Love goes both the ways where two people keep same effort.”

Carol: “How do I know if someone is in love with me?”

Pearl: “You just know it.”

Carol: “How?”

Pearl: "When they be there with you through thick and thin."

Amber: "When they meet you half way."

Pearl: "When they never leave you alone no matter what happens."

Amber: "And it's all about understanding each other."

Carol: "Tell me more about love. I want to know it."

Pearl: "Love is patient."

Amber: "Love is kind."

Pearl: "Love is eternal."

Amber: "Love makes you do impossible things."

Pearl: "Love gives you hope."

Amber: "It lights up your world."

Pearl: "It makes you fall in love with yourself everyday."

Carol: "Now I know what love is. Thank you friends. I love you guys so much. And I am hoping that we all get such love in our lives."

Pearl and Amber together: "We love you too Carol."
(Everyone hugs and goes to sleep)

STORY 6: WALKING AWAY

Carol: "What is the bravest thing you ever did in love?"

Pearl: "I walked away." (Says while building the sand castle)

Carol: "Is it not hard?"

Pearl: "Yes, it is."

Carol: "It must've been painful."

Pearl: "More than you can imagine."

Carol: "Didn't you love him?"

Pearl: "I did."

Carol: "Then?"

Pearl: "Sometimes love is not enough to be in a relationship."

Carol: "What else do we need ?"

Pearl: "Respect, loyalty and effort."

Carol: “Is it that important. I thought if there’s love then there will be respect, loyalty and trust.”

Pearl: “It’s not necessary to have all that if there’s love. Sometimes all that takes back seat when love blindsides you.”

Carol: “How do we know that?”

Pearl: “If someone loves you truly they won’t make you second guess your worth and doesn’t make you feel unloved. That’s respect.”

Carol: “Then what’s loyalty?”

Pearl: “If someone truly loves you they won’t choose someone over you. They will not replace you.”

Carol: “Then what is an effort?”

Pearl: “If they love you they will not put all the baggage of the relationship on you, they will try to meet you halfway in everything.”

Carol: “Woah! That’s deep!”

Pearl: “Yes.”

Carol: “Did you lose all that in your relationship?”

Pearl: “Hmm yes, I did. I lost myself.”

Carol: “What did you do then?”

Pearl: “I found myself again.”

Carol: "How did you do it?"

Pearl: "It was not easy. But I chose me and that showed me the way."

Carol: "Isn't that selfish?"

Pearl: "No, it isn't. You can't lose yourself just because you love someone."

Carol: "Isn't that all women do?"

Pearl: "Yes we do, and that is wrong. You can't dissolve yourself in love. Love should make you stronger not weak. If your love is making you weak and you don't know who you are anymore. Then you should let go of it."

Carol: "It's not easy right."

Pearl: "Yes, it's not easy. But it's not worth to be at a place where you don't have respect, where you are not treated well. If there's no respect there's no love."

Carol: "I get it now."

Pearl: "Someone raising hand on you is an abuse, but sometimes not giving you respect is also an abuse. Many women don't understand that."

Carol: "So abuse can be silent too."

Pearl: "Yes, It is."

Carol: "That's when we should walk away?"

Pearl: " Yes, and that's what I did."

Carol: "You are so brave."

Pearl: "Pain made me brave."
(Amber comes home from shopping)

Amber: "That's why mom says that walking away from someone who is hurting you for a long time is brave."

Pearl: "Yes, that's right."

Carol: "Amberrrr!"
(Carol goes and hugs Amber)

Pearl joins them.

STORY 7: NOT A LOVE

Carol: "How do you know if someone truly loves you?"

Pearl: "You just know it."

Carol: " Tell me how?"

Amber: " I will tell you. For that you should know what is not love before you know what is love."

Carol: "Oh! So what is not love?"

Amber: "If someone wants you, but doesn't want to marry you, that's not love."

Carol: "Whaaaaat?"

Amber: "When someone keeps you on standby and gives you excuses even to spend time with you, that's not love."

Carol: "Is it?"

Amber: "Yes my dear someone can be busy, but not that busy where they can't call you or text you in 24 hours.

Carol: "I see. I didn't knew it."

Amber: Yes darling, Someone can love you madly, but if they hurt you that's not love."

Carol "Oh my god."

Amber: Someone can love you deeply, but if they always keep you as a secret then that's not love."

Carol: "What else is not love."

Amber: "When someone tells you that they love you but doesn't want to walk in front of others by holding your hand then that's not love,

when someone yells at you then that's not love,

when someone breaks things just to prove their point then that's not love,

when someone doesn't put you first then that's not love,

when someone constantly makes you feel anxious then that's not love,

when someone doesn't want to discuss life with you but wants to make love to you then that's not love,

when someone makes you beg them for bare minimum things then that's not love,

not fighting for you is not love,
not standing up for you is not love,
not taking care of you is not love,
not apologizing to you is not love,
not letting you speak is not love,
not letting you wear a dark lipstick is not love,

not letting you wear what you like is not love,
not letting you decide what you want is not love,
and sometimes silence is also not love."

Carol: " That's scary."

Amber: "You know what's the scariest part?"

Carol: "What is it?"

Amber: "When they take control over your life even before you know it."

Carol: "Does that really happen?"

Amber: "Yes it does. When they make you apologize even when it's not your mistake, when they give you love only when it is convenient for them, when they always make you crave for their attention, when they make you believe that they are busy and gives you only little time, when they never appreciate you for what you do and expects more, that's not love."

Carol: "I never thought of it like this."

Amber: "Yes we never and that's why we get hurt."

Carol: "I will never let anyone do that with me."

Amber: "Yeah, you be careful."

Carol: "I will be."

Amber: "Sometimes pain can be disguised as love and it can occupy your entire life, but you should sense it form a mile away."

Carol: “How?”

Amber: “It’s all in the little details, you just have to observe how the other person is treating you.”

Carol: “Okay, I will do that.”

Amber: "You know, Mom says 'If someone loves you truly, they will fight for you and they will never make you feel unloved, even for a second.'”

Carol: “Okay I understood now.”

Amber: “I’m glad you did.”

(Carol sips her tea confidently)

STORY 8: DARKNESS

Carol: "How can I come out of the darkness?"

Pearl: "You have to find a way, Carol."

Carol: “How can I find the way?”

Pearl: “You have to look for the light.”

Carol: “After that?”

Pearl: “You have to walk towards it.”

Carol: “That’s it?”

Pearl: “Yes.”

Carol: “What if I don’t find the light?”

Pearl: “You just keep looking for it until you find it.”

Carol: “Then?”

Pearl: “Then the light will kill the darkness.”

Carol: “Where can I find this light?”

Pearl: "It is there everywhere around you."

Carol: "What! Everywhere, seriously?"

Pearl: "Yes."

Carol: "Can I find it in a place?"

Pearl: "Yes, and also inside people."

Carol: "That's interesting."

Pearl: "You know what's more interesting?"

Carol: "What?"

Pearl: "It is there even inside you."

Carol: "Inside me?"

Pearl: "Yes."

Carol: "But I don't see it."

Pearl: "You can't, but you can see it if you find it."

Carol: "How do I find it?"

Pearl: "Just make the right choices."

Carol: "Like what?"

Pearl: "Don't hurt others,

don't hurt yourself,

know when to stay and when to let go,
know what to tolerate and what to not,
know what is worth fighting for,

take stand for what you believe,
don't be afraid to let go anything,
help others,
help yourself,

be there for yourself,
be empathetic,
above all be kind to others and yourself."

Carol: "So I'm the light?"

Pearl: "Yes you are."

Carol: "Thank you Pearl for telling me this. I will start looking for the light inside me."

Pearl: "Good luck on that, my girl!"

Amber: "What's happening girls? Did I miss something?"

Carol: "Pearl just told me how to find inner light."

Amber: "That's so nice of you pearl. You know Mom says you can come out of darkness only when you walk towards the light. Sometimes, you can find that light in the people you love, and sometimes it's already there inside you; you just have to find it, Carol."

Carol: " Sure, I will."

STORY 9: UNREQUITED LOVE

Carol: “Pearl, can I ask you something?”

Pearl: “Yes, you can.”

Carol: “What is unrequited love?”

Pearl: “Why do you want to know, Carol?”

Carol: “Please tell me Pearl. I want to know.”

Pearl: “ Uh uh. Okay. When you love someone and they don’t love you back. That’s unrequited love.”

Carol: “Oh. You mean one sided?”

Pearl: “Yes, exactly.”

Carol: “But I have a question. Why he don’t love me back even when I love him more?”

Pearl: “It depends on his feelings.”

Carol: “But he knows that I love him right.”

Pearl: “Yes, and still he might choose not to love you.”

Carol: "But he talks to me all the time right."

Pearl: "Yes he can talk but not love you."

Carol: "He cares about me."

Pearl: "He can care about you, but still not love you."

Carol: "He fights with me all the time."

Pearl: "He likes fighting with you, but still not love you."

Carol: "He texts me all the time."

Pearl: "He can text, but still not love you."

Carol: "Then what should I do?"

Pearl: "You just leave him alone. If he loves you he will come to you."

Carol: "Sometimes he goes silent for days."

Pearl: "Why would he do that?"

Carol: "Just to keep me away."

Pearl: "That's concerning."

Pearl: "Did you tell him that he is hurting you?"

Carol: "Yes I did."

Pearl: "What did he say?"

Carol: "He says sorry. But he does it again."

Pearl: "You don't have to accept his behavior just because you love him, Carol. Love isn't supposed to scare you."

Carol: "Sometimes I feel I'm not worthy."

Pearl: "No Carol, it's not true. You are worthy of everything and you deserve all the love in this world."

Carol: "But I feel so unloved."

Pearl: "Carol, you are feeling like that because you are searching for love in wrong places. Sometimes what you find cannot be the love you want."

Carol: " Is it?"

Pearl: "Yes, it is. Sometimes we like someone and we want to know about them and we want to be with them. We think it's love, but sometimes it can be our stubbornness too which makes us want the impossible."

Carol: "I felt bad when he said no. But I had hope."

Pearl: "See you know he has no feelings for you but you waited for him with unrealistic expectations."

Carol: "Yeah I shouldn't have done that."

Pearl: "It happens Carol. We all go through such phase in life. But you have to realize that he is not the one for you. He can't give you what you want. Love should be easy, it doesn't happen if you force someone."

Carol: "I understood now Pearl."

Pearl: "I'm glad you did. When someone doesn't have feelings for you, let it be. If they don't love you, let it be. But don't get hurt in that process. Don't give importance to someone and put them first. You should keep yourself and your self respect first. Everything comes after that."

Carol: "What if I don't find love again?"

Pearl: One day you will find it. Just have faith."

Carol: "So I shouldn't wait for this man?"

Pearl: "No, you shouldn't. Because you gave him chance and he hurt you to the core, so you shouldn't give a second chance again. Because it is okay if you be single forever, but you can't be with someone who hurts you just because you love him. It's not good for you."

Carol: "Okay Pearl, thank you for telling me this. It means a lot."

(Carol hugs Pearl)

STORY 10: DREAM

Carol: "Do dreams come true?"

Pearl: "Yes, they do."

Amber: “Only if you chase them.”

Carol: “ Sometimes I get scared.”

Pearl: “Why?”

Carol: “I feel like I’m not doing much in life and I’m far away from my dream.”

Amber: “That’s not true Carol.”

Pearl: “You are working very hard and we all know it.”

Carol: “Yes, but I’m not happy inside. I feel like I’m doing injustice to my dream.”

Pearl: “What is your dream Carol.”

Carol: “I want to become a singer.”

Amber: “Wow Carol. That’s amazing.”

Pearl: " I didn't know you have such big dream. I always loved your voice."

Carol: Thank you Pearl. I love singing from a young age, but I was scared to sing in front of others."

Pearl: "So where do you sing then?"

Carol: "Promise me you won't laugh."

Amber: "Promise Carol. We will not laugh."

Pearl: "Yeah, promise."

Carol: "I sing in bathroom while taking shower."

Pearl: "Ohh that's great."

Amber: "Is that you who disturbs my sleep every morning? I though it's our neighbor's radio and cursed them many a times."

Carol: "No, that's me."

Pearl: "You should join music school then and practice vocals."

Amber: "Yeah and you should practice everyday, Carol."

Carol: "But I'm not finding time and my parents don't like it. They think it's waste of time and they want me to do a 9 to 5 job."

Pearl: "No Carol, that's not waste of time. You should do what you love."

Amber: "You won't be happy if you don't pursue your dream."

Carol: "I'm struggling in-between my job and my dream."

Pearl: "You can do your job and can still pursue your dream."

Carol: "Is it?"

Pearl: "Yes Carol, there is always a way. You just have to find it."

Amber: "You can do your 9 to 5 job and can practice singing in your free time everyday."

Pearl: "You can also practice even on weekends."

Carol: "Yeah, why didn't I think of it."

Pearl: "You just need a proper schedule."

Carol: "Yes I will start working on it from today."

Amber: "Will you remember us if you become a great singer?"

Carol: "Of course Amber, how can I forget you guys. You guys are my family."

Pearl: "So are you ready to chase your dream, Carol?

Carol: "Yes, I'm."

Amber: "Never turn back, Carol. Always keep going forward."

Carol: “Okay Amber.”

Amber: “You know, Mom says ‘If you dream of having something in your life, you just have to go after it.’”

Carol: “Aye Aye, captain.”
(Everyone laughs)

STORY 11: LETTING GO

Carol: "What is the best thing you can do for yourself?"

Pearl: "I let go."

Carol: "Letting go means?"

Pearl: "It means you should leave the things or people who no longer make you happy."

Carol: "But I'm going to lose them right."

Pearl: "Yes, but if you hold on to them they are going to make you sad."

Carol: "They also made me happy."

Pearl: "Yes, but that's in the past when everything was fine. But things don't be the same always."

Carol: "Is it?"

Pearl: "Yes, people change, situations change, habits change."

Carol: "Sounds scary."

Pearl: “Yes, love can become hate,
happiness can become sadness,
friends can become strangers,
relatives can become rivals,
peace can turn into chaos,
your strength can turn into weakness.”

Carol: “Oh my god.”

Pearl: “When things change and if it makes you sad or anxious, then you should let it go for your good.”

Carol: “But leaving people is bad right.”

Pearl: “It becomes bad when you leave a good person. But if someone is hurting you everyday and makes you feel belittle about yourself, and makes you feel like everything is your fault and isolates you then why do you want such person in your life?”

Carol: “Yes, I don’t want such a bad person in my life.”

Pearl: “So it doesn’t have to be someone you love or someone who loves you. It can be anyone.”

Carol: “So if something is hurting me I should let it go right?”

Pearl: “Yes, without any doubt.”

Carol: How do I know that exactly?”

Pearl: “If something is weighing you down everyday and makes you sad and worry about it all the time then that’s a sign that it is no longer good for you.”

Carol: "Is it even for thoughts?"

Pearl: "Yes, you live most of the time in your mind and if something bothers you constantly and if you think about it all the time and if that thought makes you feel drained emotionally, then you should let it go."

Carol: "I always think about my past, and I don't sleep properly"

Pearl: "See, that's what I was talking about. If you keep thinking about the same thing over and over again then it's not going to get changed. It has happened already in the past and you can't change anything back by thinking about it million times."

Carol: "I'm not able to forget about it?"

Pearl: "Do you think you can go back in time and change that past?"

Carol: "No."

Pearl: "Then?"

Carol: "But it just doesn't go away from my mind"

Pearl: "Do you have a time machine?"

Carol: "No."

Pearl: "Can you go back in time and change anything?"

Carol: "No."

Pearl: "Then why are you thinking about it and living in that dark loop everyday?"

Carol: "I don't know. I'm just not able to forget any of it."

Pearl: "That's what you should let go, Carol."

Carol: "Mmmm.. Maybe."

Pearl: "Your past is eating you alive everyday. You are not happy from inside. It is making you weak and stressed if you keep on holding on to it."

Carol: "Yes, it is."

Pearl: "So for your peace of mind you should stop thinking about it and let it all go."

Carol: "Yes Pearl. I will."

Pearl: "There is no good in thinking about your past. It just happened and you should leave it there. Don't carry old memories into new experiences. It only hurts."

Carol: "Yeah, I'm getting it now. I will let go of everything that's bothering me now. I will be peaceful from now onwards."

Pearl: "That's great."

(Amber comes home from office and listens everything)

Amber: "You know Carol, my mom always says that you should let go of something that hurts you over and over again and weighs you down. Sometimes happiness isn't found in holding on, but it's found in letting go."

Pearl: "See Amber agrees with me."

Carol: "Yes, I will let go of it now and I will never think of it again."

Pearl: "Promise?"

Carol: "Yes, pinky promise."

(Everyone laughs, and Carol leaves the kite she's holding in her hands and it flies away in the sky)

STORY 12: SELF-CARE

Carol: "Amber"

Amber: "Yes Carol."

Carol: "What is Self-Care?"

Amber: "It is taking care of yourself."

Carol: "I always take care of myself and my parents and friends also take care of me. I also do my Hair care, skin care and body care."

Amber: "It taking care of what's inside you, your inner self Carol, not just the outer self."

Carol: "How can I take care of it then?"

Amber: "By choosing what is healthy for you. By making conscious choices."

Carol: "How do I know that?"

Amber: "You should just start by focusing on what you are feeding for your mind, body and soul. Also observe how you are treating yourself."

Carol: "Is it okay to do it one day?"

Amber: "No Carol, you should do it everyday."

Carol: "Everyday! Seriously?"

Amber: "Yes Carol. Self-Care is an everyday process."

Carol: "Okay, teach me."

Amber: "You have to be very careful about how you perceive the things, what you speak to yourself, how you think about yourself and how you be there for yourself."

Carol: "So I have to be a detective then?"

Amber: "Of course Carol. You have to keep check on your heart, mind and soul every day. You should see if the people around and the place you are in are good for you or not. You should see if you are in a right place among right people. The people you choose, the people you hang out with impacts your personality and perspective, the way you think and the way you act also affects by your surroundings."

Carol: "I never thought of it."

Amber: "You should Carol."

Pearl: "And you have to be careful."

Carol: "I will from now onwards."

Amber: "Don't let negative people get into your head. Some people just talk about your flaws only to demotivate you."

Pearl: "And if they don't find any flaws they just create them."

Carol: "That's wrong, isn't it?"

Amber: "Yes, it is."

Pearl: "That's why you shouldn't let anyone get into your head."

Carol: "Okay Pearl. I will not believe them. I will trust myself. "

Amber: "And you should trust your instincts."

Pearl: "Because it never lies."

Carol: "Okay, and then?"

Amber: "Then what, you just go and enjoy your life."

Carol: "Wohoooo!'

(Carol gets up and runs outside, pearl goes to catch her)

STORY 13: MENTAL HEALTH

Pearl: "Amber, have you seen Carol?"

Amber: "No. She must be in her room."

Pearl: "I just checked she isn't anywhere."

Amber: "Where she must have gone? Did you say something to her?"

Pearl: "No Amber. I didn't say anything to her. Why would I do that."

Amber: "Then what made her disappear so suddenly?"

Pearl: "No idea."

Amber: "Have you checked in the drawing room."

Pearl: "Yes, she is not there in the drawing room."

Amber: Have you checked in the garden area."

Pearl: "Yes. But no luck."

Amber: "Have you checked the pool area?"

Pearl: "Yes, but it's empty."

Amber: "Have you checked in the attic?"

Pearl: "No. I forgot to check there, sorry."

Amber: "Okay. Let's go and check in the attic."
(They both climb to the attic. They see Carol crying in a corner)

Pearl: "Amber, she's crying."
(Amber goes to Carol)

Amber: "What happened Carol, why are you crying? Are you okay?"

Carol: "I'm okay."

Pearl: "Then why are you crying?"

Carol: "It's nothing."

Amber: "There has to be a reason."

Carol: "No, nothing."

Pearl: "Then what made you sad?"

Carol: "I sometimes feel like crying."

Amber: "Why haven't you told me this before? Pearl do you know about this?"

Pearl: "No Amber. She never told me about this."

Carol: "Pearl knows nothing about this Amber."

Amber: "What else do you feel?"

Carol: "I sometimes feel low. I feel like I'm nothing."

Pearl: "No, you are not."

Amber: "And what else do you feel?"

Carol: "Sometimes I get angry and feels like breaking things."

Amber: "And?"

Carol: "And I feel like I'm lonely and nothing excites me."

Amber: "Why do you feel like that?"

Pearl: "But you were always happy with us and it never felt like you are sad."

Carol: "Yes, when I'm with you guys. You make me feel happy and most of the times I pretend that I'm happy."

Amber: "Why haven't you talk to us about this?"

Carol: "I was scared that you would judge me."

Pearl: "No Carol. We would never do that."

Amber: "We will never judge you Carol. We will accept you as you are."

Carol: "I thought you guys will make fun of me."

Pearl: "No, never."

Amber: "Oh love! you have misunderstood us. We would never judge you or laugh at you. You can talk to us anytime. We are always ready to listen to you."

Carol: "Is it true?"

Amber: "Yes dear.
(Amber hugs Carol)

Pearl: "Yes Carol. We are always with you."
(Pearl goes to Carol and holds her hand)

Amber: "Now tell me what else do you feel?"

Carol: "Sometimes I get shivering. My heart beat increases and I feel like I am sinking deep into something."

Pearl: "Something like what?"

Carol: "No idea."

Amber: "Like darkness?"

Carol: "Maybe."

Pearl: "Do you have any tiredness?"

Carol: "Yes, I feel tired sometimes. And I feel empty in my stomach and I can't breathe properly sometimes."

Amber: "Oh poor girl! Why haven't you come to us then?"

Pearl: "I'm sorry you had to go through that all alone."

Carol: "I just didn't wanted to burden you guys."

Amber: "No Carol, you are never a burden to us."

Pearl: "Remember we are a family."

Carol: "Yes, we are a family."

Amber: "When did all this start?"

Carol: "I suddenly started feel like this from the past few months. I sometimes feel like hurting myself."

Amber: "Oh Carol! This looks like depression."

Pearl: "Yeah. It sounds like that."

Carol: "Is it bad to feel like this?"

Amber: "No, it's not Carol. It is okay cry. It is okay to let it out. And it is okay to be not okay."

Pearl: "Yes, it is okay to feel this way."

Amber: "It is okay to ask help."

Pearl: "It is okay to let it all out."

Amber: "It's just a phase and you can come out of it."

Carol: "How can I come out of it? I don't want to be depressed like this anymore."

Amber: "You know Carol, the first step towards healing is thinking to come out of it and you already took that first step."

Carol: “What is the next step?”

Pearl: “You keep trying to come out of it everyday.”

Carol: “But how?”

Amber: “You should choose happiness everyday.”

Pearl: “You should start seeing positive side in everything.”

Amber: “By maintaining a routine.”

Pearl: “You should go on a morning walk.”

Amber: “You should do meditation.”

Pearl: “You should take deep breaths.”

Amber: “Do the things you love.”

Carol: “Like coloring?”

Amber: “Yes, exactly. And you can also sing.”

Pearl: “You can also cook and travel a lot.”

Carol: “But I never gone anywhere outside.”

Amber: “That is why you are feeling like this. You should go out frequently and meet people and explore the world.”

Pearl: “Yes, and you should read books too.”

Carol: “Okay.

Amber: “And you should go for a therapy too.”

Carol: "Therapy? I don't want to go."

Pearl: "Why you don't want to go?"

Amber: "What are you afraid of?"

Carol: "Doc will judge me."

Pearl: "No Carol, Doc will never judge you. In fact he listens to you and helps you to heal."

Amber: "Yes Carol, what we told you to do is a part of self care. But you also need to take professional help to heal completely.

Carol: "I'm okay Amber. You guys are there to help me. I don't need others."

Amber: "But we are not professionals. We can only help you till certain point. But the doc can understand you way better and guide you properly."

Pearl: "Yes, and you don't have to do it alone. We will be right there with you outside the door. "

Carol: "Really."

Amber: "Yes Carol. We will come with you."

Carol: "You guys are the best. "

Pearl: "Healing is a journey Carol. And we love to be a part of your journey."

Amber: "And whenever you feel like hurting yourself again you should come to us first. Will you Carol?"

Carol: "Yes Amber. I will come to you guys."

Pearl: "Your are so brave Carol."

Amber: "And we love you."

Carol: "I love you too guys."

Amber: "Okay I'm taking doc's appointment tomorrow at 10 am. Just be ready."

Carol: " Okay Amber. If you don't mind can you guys sleep with me today in my room?"
Amber and Pearl: "Of course, we would love to."
(Amber tucks Carol in bed and sleeps next to her. Pearl jumps in. They all hug each other and slowly Carol goes to sleep)

STORY 14: HOPE

Carol: "I give up, guys. My life isn't going anywhere. I'm so tired of trying it over and over again."

Pearl: "That's not true, my love. Everything is just in your head. You are going in the right direction."

Carol: "But I feel stuck and my life is not moving."

Amber: "You are just overthinking, Carol."

Pearl: "You know, sometimes it takes longer than usual to reach your goals, but you need to wait with patience."

Amber: "That's when you shouldn't feel disappointed. Instead of overthinking about how you are reaching your goal, see your everyday victories, all the steps you have taken to reach till now."

Pearl: "Yes, every step counts."

Carol: "Sometimes I feel I'm not at the right place too."
Amber: "No love, you are exactly where you are supposed to be."

Pearl: "Even if you can't see it now, later you will realize that you were meant to be here and all this was worth it."

Carol: "But I don't see any change in my life."

Amber: "You know, Mom says, 'Just because you don't see any change happening in your life, it doesn't mean nothing is happening. Your life is better than yesterday and you are in a better place than where you were last year.'"

Carol: "Yeah."

Pearl: "Sometimes good things happen to us Carol, but you don't notice them while worrying about the things that are not in your control."

Amber: "Worrying only makes your life more miserable."

Carol: "I worry so much about everything."

Amber: "The more you worry about everything around you, the more you tangle your life."

Carol: "How can I come out of it.

Pearl: "You should stop worrying and start to be optimistic about everything."

Amber: "You have to change the perspective of how you look at the things."

Carol: "But what if I lose again?"

Pearl: "It is okay to lose, Carol."

Amber: "There is always a next time for everything. If you lose now, you can win later. All you have to do is keep working hard and not think about the result, because all that matters is your effort."

Carol: "Okay, so does that mean I can try as many times as possible."

Pearl: "Yes, you can."

Amber: "You can try as many times as possible Carol. But you shouldn't give up so easily. "

Carol: "Sometimes life feel so hard?"

Pearl: "It's not as hard as you think, Carol."

Amber: "You know, mom says 'Life is beautiful, but our thoughts can make it difficult. If we think we have everything, then we have everything in our lives. If we think we have nothing, then we have nothing in our lives."

Pearl: "You need to have hope."

Carol: "What is hope?"

Pearl: "It's a feeling and you can't see it."

Carol: "Do I have it inside me?"

Pearl: "Yes, you do."

Amber: "We all have it inside us, and the world runs on hope."

Pearl: “Whenever you feel like nothing is working out and nothing is happening just remember that everything works out in the end.”

Carol: “Is it?”

Pearl: “Yes, that’s true.”

Amber: “And, you know, mom says that no matter what you’re going through right now, no matter how hard life is, you get a feeling inside that tells you everything gets better in the end. That feeling is hope.”

Carol: “Now I got it. And I will not give up again.”

Pearl: “You better not.”

Amber: “Never lose your hope Carol. Keep fighting back.”

Carol: “I will Amber.”

Pearl: “I hope the cookies I baked tastes good”

Carol: “ Of course.”

Amber: “See that’s hope.”
(Everyone laughs while looking at the sunrise from their window)

STORY 15: HEALING

Carol: "How can I pretend I'm fine when I'm actually not?"

Pearl: "You just have to smile I guess."

Amber: "Why do you want to pretend Carol?"

Carol: "I have lost so much in this past one year and I don't feel happy inside and I feel lonely all the time even in crowd."

Pearl: "Oh Carol, not your drama again."

Amber: " Pearl don't be so mean. Apologize to Carol."

Carol: " It's okay Amber."

Amber: "No, it's not. Pearl, apologize now."

Pearl: "Sorry, Carol."

Amber: "Pearl, when someone comes to you to talk and discuss about their problems, you don't make fun of them. Instead you should listen to them and help them heal."

Pearl: "Does talking heal people?"

Amber: “Yes, when you let them talk they pour out their heart and let it all out and letting out emotions is the first step towards healing.”

Pearl: “I never saw it that way Amber, sorry.”

Amber: “It’s okay Pearl. Now let’s help Carol.”

Pearl: “Sure, Amber.”

Amber: “Since when you are pretending to be fine Carol?”

Carol: “Since very long time.”

Amber: “But why did you do it?”

Carol: “Because I didn’t want people to know I’m not okay.”

Amber: “But why?”

Carol: “ Because I thought it’s not okay to show them my vulnerable side. And if I show maybe people will stop loving me.”

Amber: “Oh poor Carol. That’s not true.”

Pearl: “Yes Carol, we love you even when you are not okay.”

Amber: “You know, mom says, ‘You don’t have to pretend to be fine when you are not, it is okay to be sad, it is okay to be angry, it is okay to feel lonely, it is okay to cry, it is okay to give up. Because it is okay to feel that way and nobody is going to judge you for that.’”

Carol: “So it’s okay to be not okay?”

Pearl: "Yes it is."

Amber: "You don't have to hide your pain from the world. If you hide it how can you heal yourself."

Carol: "I shouldn't have hide that from you guys."

Amber: "It's okay. We understand."

Pearl: " I agree with Amber."

Carol: "So how can I heal myself now?"

Amber: "You just have to let it all out and know that whatever happened is not your fault."

Pearl: "And you don't blame yourself everyday."

Amber: "Don't hate yourself."

Pearl: "You should stop feeling like your life is over and stop pretending that everything is okay."

Carol: "Tell me more."

Amber: "You should start interacting with people,
get out of bed and go out with friends,

talk to someone about your feelings,
maintain a daily routine,

talking to people at least for an hour should be a part of your daily routine,

call people instead of texting them, sometimes hearing the voice of a known person can be soothing.

try to make yourself busy, sometimes being idle can also cause loneliness.

start a new hobby,
go for a walk, sometimes it clears your head,

do meditation,
Above all ask for help. Because asking for help is okay and there is no need to feel ashamed."

Carol: "So that means everything is in my hands. I can heal myself?"

Pearl: "Yes, you can."

Amber: "Sometimes healing doesn't come from the outside, it often comes from within."

Pearl: "When you don't heal yourself no one can heal you."

Carol: "I have learnt a new thing today. I'm glad I came to you guys."

Amber: "So next time when you feel lonely when you feel unloved, and when you feel unimportant. Remember that we all are there with you and we love all your scars and flaws."

Pearl: "And remember to embrace all the parts of you. The happy you, the sad you, the broken you, the angry you, the lonely you. You have to embrace it all."

Carol: "Okay guys. I will concentrate more on the healing and less on my problems."

Amber and Pearl: "We are proud of you Carol."

(As they drove off on their bicycles happily, Carol feels free and changed from Inside)